五分鐘的安寧

吉爾‧墨菲

© Jill Murphy, 1986

© Chinese translation, Magi Publications, 1995

This edition published in 1995 by Magi Publications, in association with
Star Books International, 55 Crowland Avenue, Hayes, Middx UB3 4JP

First Published in Great Britain in 1986 by Walker Books Ltd, London

Printed and bound in Italy by L.E.G.O., Vicenza

ISBN 1 85430 356 2

Five Minutes' Peace

Jill Murphy

Translated by East Word

MAGI PUBLICATIONS

London

孩子們正在吃早餐。
他們的吃相不好看。

The children were having breakfast.
This was not a pleasant sight.

拉奇太太從碗櫃裡拿出一個托盤。
她把一個茶壺、一個盛牛奶用的壺、她最喜歡的茶杯、一碟子塗
上果醬的多士和昨天吃剩的蛋糕都放在托盤上。她將早報插入口
袋然後偷偷地向門的方向走去。

Mrs Large took a tray from the cupboard. She set it
with a teapot, a milk jug, her favourite cup and saucer,
a plate of marmalade toast and a leftover cake from yesterday.
She stuffed the morning paper into her pocket and sneaked
off towards the door.

"您拿著托盤去哪裡，媽媽?" 勞拉問。
"去浴室，" 拉奇太太説。
"爲甚麼呢?" 另外兩個孩子問道。
"因爲我想單獨有五分鐘的安寧，" 拉奇太太説道。
"那就是爲甚麼。"

"Where are you going with that tray, Mum?"
asked Laura.
"To the bathroom," said Mrs Large.
"Why?" asked the other two children.
"Because I want five minutes' peace from *you* lot,"
said Mrs Large. "That's why."

　　"我們也可以去嗎?" 萊斯特問道。他們排成一隊,跟在媽媽
後面也想上樓梯。

　　"不可以," 拉奇太太說, "你們不能去。"

勞拉問: "那麼我們應該做甚麼呢?"

拉奇太太說: "你們可以玩耍,在樓下你們自己玩,
並且要照顧小寶寶。"

　　"我不是小寶寶," 最小的孩子不滿地說。

"Can *we* come?" asked Lester as they trailed up the stairs behind her.

"No," said Mrs Large, "you can't."

"What shall *we* do then?" asked Laura.

"You can play," said Mrs Large. "Downstairs. By yourselves.
And keep an eye on the baby."

"I'm *not* a baby," muttered the little one.

拉奇太太往浴缸裡加滿了熱水，準備洗個熱水澡。她往水裡加了半瓶的浴液，戴上她的浴帽，然後進了浴缸。她爲自己倒了一杯茶，然後閉上眼睛往後躺了下來。
這簡直是天堂。

Mrs Large ran a deep, hot bath. She emptied half a bottle of bath-foam into the water, plonked on her bath-hat and got in. She poured herself a cup of tea and lay back with her eyes closed. It was heaven.

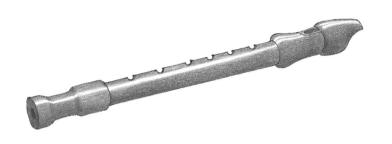

"我可以爲你表演我的豎笛嗎?" 萊斯特問。
拉奇太太睜開了一隻眼睛,說: "你一定要表演嗎?"
"我一直在練習吹笛," 萊斯特說。 "是你告訴我要練習的。
我能吹給你聽嗎? 讓我吹一下吧,我只吹一分鐘。"
"那就吹吧," 拉奇太太嘆了口氣。 萊斯特就吹起了他的豎笛。
他吹的一曲 『閃爍、閃爍小星星』 吹了三次半。

"Can I play you my tune?" asked Lester.
Mrs Large opened one eye. "Must you?" she asked.
"I've been practising," said Lester. "You told me to. *Can* I?
Please, just for *one* minute."
"Go *on* then," sighed Mrs Large. So Lester played. He played
"Twinkle, Twinkle, Little Star" three and a half times.

勞拉走了進來，她問：“我可以爲你朗讀一頁我在看的書嗎?”

“不行，勞拉，”拉奇太太説。“出去，你們都下樓去。”

“但你讓萊斯特吹豎笛，”勞拉説。“我聽到了他吹。你偏心、你更喜歡他，這不公平。”

“勞拉，別傻想了。”拉奇太太説。“那你讀吧，但只讀一頁。”

勞拉就開始朗讀了。她足足讀了四頁半的『小紅帽』。

In came Laura. "Can I read you a page from my reading book?" she asked.

"*No, Laura,*" said Mrs Large. "Go on, *all* of you, off downstairs."

"You let Lester play his tune," said Laura. "I heard.
You like him better than me. It's not fair."

"Oh, don't be silly, Laura," said Mrs Large. "Go *on* then.
Just *one* page." So Laura read. She read four and half pages of "Little Red Riding Hood".

小寶寶抱著滿滿一箱的玩具走了進來。

"這些是給你的!" 他顯得興致勃勃,一下子把全部玩具統統
扔進浴缸的水中。

拉奇太太無可奈何地說:"謝謝你,親愛的。"

In came the little one with a trunkful of toys.
"For *you*!" he beamed, flinging them all into the bath water.
"Thank you, dear," said Mrs Large weakly.

勞拉問: "我能看報紙上的連環圖嗎?"
萊斯特問: "我能吃蛋糕嗎?"
小寶寶問: "我能進浴缸裡和你在一起嗎?" 拉奇太太嘆了口氣。

"Can I see the cartoons in the paper?" asked Laura.
"Can I have the cake?" asked Lester.
"Can I get in with you?" asked the little one. Mrs Large groaned.

他們全都進了浴缸裡。小寶寶太性急，連睡衣都
忘了脫。

In the end they *all* got in. The little one was in such a hurry
that he forgot to take off his pyjamas.

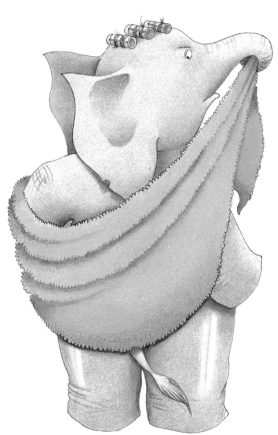

拉奇太太走出了浴缸。她擦干了身體，穿上浴袍
然後向門邊走去。
"你去哪裡，媽媽?" 勞拉問。
"去廚房，" 拉奇太太説。
"爲甚麽呢?" 萊斯特問。
"因爲我想單獨有五分鐘的安寧，" 拉奇太太説。
"那就是爲什麽。"

Mrs Large got out. She dried herself, put on her
dressing-gown and headed for the door.
"Where are you going *now*, Mum?" asked Laura.
"To the kitchen," said Mrs Large.
"Why?" asked Lester.
"Because I want five minutes' peace from *you* lot,"
said Mrs Large. "That's why."

她離開了浴室下了樓，在那裡她只享受到了
三分零四十五秒的安寧，然後孩子們又來和她
'團圓' 了。

And off she went downstairs, where she
had three minutes and forty-five seconds of
peace before they all came to join her.